3 Toes

MESALAND
SERIES

Stories by LOYD TIREMAN

Adapted by EVELYN YRISARRI

Layout and Illustrations
By RALPH DOUGLASS

A Facsimile of the 1949 First Edition

University of New Mexico Press   Albuquerque

2015 edition published by arrangement with Marilyn D. Carlson.
Printed in China

20 19 18 17 16 15   1 2 3 4 5 6

LIBRARY OF CONGRESS CATALOGING-IN-PUBLICATION DATA

Tireman, L. S. (Loyd Spencer), 1896–1959, author.
3 toes / stories by Loyd Tireman ; adapted by Evelyn Yrisarri ; layout
and illustrations by Ralph Douglass.
    pages cm. — (Mesaland Series ; Book 7)
"A facsimile of the 1949 first edition."
Summary: "Introduces the coyote named 3 Toes, a dangerous new
face on the mesa"— Provided by publisher.
ISBN 978-0-8263-5610-9 (cloth : alk. paper) [1. Coyote—Fiction.
2. Desert animals—Fiction.] I. Yrisarri, Evelyn, adaptor. II. Douglass,
Ralph, illustrator. III. Title. IV. Title: Three toes.
PZ7.T5167Aad 2015
[E]—dc23
                    2015006378

A New Face on the Mesa

"My! my!, Hop-A-Long," said the little lady cottontail, "I think you are very, very brave. Aren't you afraid to stop and talk to me?"

"Why, no," replied Hop-A-Long. "This is a pleasure."

"Can't you hear that dog howling?" asked Cottontail, anxiously. "I'm sure it is following your tracks."

"Oh, yes, I hear him," scoffed Hop-A-Long. "But that's only Towser, the dog from the Brown

Ranch. He isn't very smart. Besides, he can't run very fast. And if by any chance he should get too close, I'll kick him with my big strong hind legs!"

"But that doesn't sound just like a dog," insisted Cottontail as she began edging toward the door to her den.

Hop-A-Long listened intently. "No, that doesn't sound exactly like Towser." The big Jack Rabbit listened again, then scrambled up the side of the arroyo to the rim where he could get a better view. "It's a Coyote!" he shouted. "And Coyotes are too smart for me. Good-bye!" Hop-A-Long didn't linger longer. He jumped away as fast as his long legs would carry him.

The Coyote appeared, looking very much like a young collie dog. He had a big bushy tail, alert

ears, and a brownish coat. His bright eyes viewed everything with caution and suspicion. He had come wandering to the mesa from his home near the foothills. He was always searching for food and adventure.

The Coyote hadn't seen the rabbits until Hop-A-Long appeared at the edge of the arroyo. Instinctively, he started to leap after Hop-A-Long, then checked himself.

"I won't chase that Rabbit," thought the Coyote. "I'll just watch him and see where he goes."

So the Coyote went up to the top of the hill where he had a good view. He didn't have to wait very long, for Hop-A-Long was afraid of the narrow arroyo. He ran out to the mesa as soon as he could.

"Someday," thought the Coyote, "I'll be waiting for Mr. Jack Rabbit in that arroyo."

Just then a dog some distance away began barking. The Coyote faced in that direction.

"I wonder," the Coyote mused to himself, "just how dangerous that dog is? It won't take me long to find out," he decided.

The Coyote cut across the sandy arroyo, then made a wide circle out over the mesa, which brought him back to his starting point.

"Yip, yip, yip," came the excited barking of Towser, for he had found the Coyote's trail.

"Now, we shall see if that dog is smart," the Coyote thought. "Let's see if he can tell an old trail from a fresh one. And if so, where the fresh one starts."

Delighted with his cleverness, the Coyote ran back up the hill. From there he could watch his whole trail. "This is better than chasing that rabbit," he thought. "It's fun playing tricks on the other animals. Besides, I learn a great deal about their habits."

Towser came into sight, barking with delight.

He had found the Coyote's tracks crossing the arroyo. He followed them in the wide circle which ran out onto the mesa. The dog didn't notice the fresh tracks going up the hill and continued going around the circle. This pleased the Coyote very much. He wrinkled up his nose in disgust with the dog.

"That fat dog will follow the circle all day,"

he laughed. "I'll never need to be afraid of him. He can't even tell old tracks from fresh ones."

The Coyote went on his way, still chuckling at the trick he had played on Towser. As he wandered along, he noticed many grasshoppers, mice, bugs, and other rabbits. "This looks like it would be a good place to live," he thought to himself. "There is lots of food. Yes," he decided, "this is just the place. Now, I'd better start looking for a good place for my den."

My, how unhappy the smaller animals were, when they heard that a coyote had come to live on their mesa!

A Day of Surprises

The Coyote was running up a wide shallow arroyo. Suddenly he stopped and sniffed, for there was a most delightful scent. His quivering nose tested the air in every direction.

"I smell a bird," he declared. Again he sniffed. The scent was faint but definite. The Coyote moved a few feet to the left.

"Ummmmmmm. The scent is much stronger here." The big fellow looked all around very carefully. "But I can't see a single bird." He was

very puzzled. "All I can see are a few rocks and a few clumps of grass."

For the third time he sniffed the air carefully. "Where can they be hidden? I definitely smell birds, yet I can't see a single one." The coyote began to move again.

The ground exploded! There was a whirring of wings. Quail flew away to the right, to the left, in front of him, and in back of him. Everywhere birds were in the air. The quail had been feeding and when the Coyote came close, they were frightened. The whole covey of quail had flown into the air at the same time.

"My goodness," said the startled Coyote. "Where did they come from?"

You see, the Coyote hadn't been able to find the birds because quail are almost the same color as the sand and rocks. That makes it very easy for them to hide.

This was the first time the big fellow had ever seen quail, so he crouched to watch them. "That's interesting," he thought. "They fly a little distance and light on the ground. Then they scurry away with little quick steps." The Coyote was so fascinated with these strange birds that he didn't try to catch any of them. "I still can't understand why I couldn't see them," he grumbled to himself. In a moment the quail had disappeared entirely before the amazed Coyote.

Close by was another shallow arroyo. The Coyote shook his head in disgust, went up the arroyo and cut across the mesa. Again he noticed the scent of birds. This time the Coyote sat down on his haunches and studied every inch of the ground. He looked at every clump of grass and every rock near by.

"Those rocks are too small," he thought. "They couldn't possibly hide a quail. And the grass around here is too straggly," he continued. "A flea couldn't hide in it. Where can they be this time?" he wondered. The Coyote blinked his eyes several times. But that didn't seem to help him see the birds any better. Finally he became impatient. "To think a small animal like a quail can outsmart me," he said. "I'll not waste any more time with them." With this remark he trotted off in a huff.

As the Coyote ran along, he happened to brush against a clump of grass. Instantly there was a whir of wings! A horned lark zoomed into

the air. The startled Coyote stopped. "How
could a bird hide in that clump of grass?" he
thought.

Sticking his nose into the clump, the Coyote
found the bird's nest. And in the nest were three
tiny baby larks.

"Baby birds are certainly ugly," he thought.
But his thought was interrupted by the Mother
Lark. She was worried about the safety of her
babies. She flew low over the nest hoping to
lure the Coyote away. As she came near, the
big animal made a lurch for her. But she was
too quick for him and turned to one side.

Just then a bullet whizzed by the Coyote's ear. This was followed by the loud "Bang" of a gun. A cowboy from the Brown Ranch had discovered the animal. The Coyote had been so busy watching the birds that he had forgotten to keep a sharp lookout for his own safety. When he heard the gun he knew his life was in danger. So off he darted, zig-zagging from side to side. The bullets kept flying,

— — — **bang,**

— — — — — — **bang,**

— — — — — **bang,**

— — — — — — — — — — — — **bang,**

but his speed and zig-zagging made him hard
to hit. Running swiftly down a rocky slope, the

Coyote stepped on a loose pebble. He fell head over heels, hitting his head on a rock. He hit so hard that he was stunned. He lay very still and didn't move. The cowboy thought he had killed the Coyote. So he stopped shooting.

It wasn't a moment until the Coyote recovered. He looked up and saw the cowboy coming toward him. "I must run," thought the frightened Coyote. And with a bound he was off like a streak of lightning. My, how surprised the cowboy was when he saw the Coyote running. Quickly he jerked up his gun. But it was too late. The animal was disappearing over the hill.

"I should have known better," grumbled the cowboy, "especially with an animal as sly as the coyote."

That evening, back at the Ranch, the cowboy told Mr. Brown about the incident. "I believe that coyote played a trick on me."

"Yes, he might have," replied Mr. Brown. "Coyotes are very smart animals. From now on we will have to watch carefully for him."

"The lambs will be in danger as long as that Coyote is around," warned the cowboy.

"Carry your guns whenever you are on the mesa," Mr. Brown commanded all the cowboys. "I want that Coyote killed."

Day after day the cowboys watched, but the Coyote was too smart and fast for them.

"I think that Coyote can smell a gun," complained one of the cowboys. "I can't get within a half mile of him when I have a rifle."

"Same with me," answered another disgusted cowboy. "But when I forget my gun, he lets me ride up close, then seems to laugh at me!"

How the Coyote Got the Name of Three Toes

When the days get short and the cold winter wind chills the mesa, the real troubles of the meat-eating animals begin. "The grasshoppers are all dead," grumbled the Coyote, "and the mice stay in their dens." He was forced to hunt long and skillfully to find any food.

So far the dog-like animal had found enough to keep him alive, but his ribs were showing. "I need meat and lots of it," he realized, as he gnawed on an old bone. "If I don't find some

soon, I must try to steal a lamb." He shivered
at the thought, for the sheep herder was watch-
ful, and moreover, he had two fierce dogs.

"This bone only makes me hungrier," snarled
the coyote. He started across the mesa as quietly
as the shadow of a floating cloud. Each clump
of grass was examined. Every mouse hole was
investigated for even a bit would be welcome.

Then he paused. "Do I smell food, or am I so hungry that I just imagine I do?" he thought. The Happy Breezes were trying to tell him something, but what? He swung his head from side to side, searching for the scent. Sometimes it came a little clearer. He crept around a little hill. "Yes, there is meat near by. I think it is a dead sheep." He went faster, for his hunger was

drawing him. He saw it. "A whole sheep!" he
gasped. It would keep him alive for a long time.
He went down the hill with a rush.

Then the Coyote stopped. He had not earned
the name of "the cleverest hunter on the mesa"
by being foolish. "Can this be a trap?" he
asked himself. He looked all around. "I don't
see any tracks of Man." He made a wide detour.
"I don't smell any Man scent." He sniffed on
all sides for he felt very uneasy.

The rich scent of the dead sheep drove him half-crazy. In spite of his fears his legs carried him near the tempting food. He came closer, then sank to the ground and crawled. One foot reached out ahead and he drew himself up— then another foot went out. He just inched along. And, as it happened, he crawled safely between two steel traps hidden in the sand.

Finally the Coyote could touch the sheep. His hunger was almost beyond control. He gave one more quick glance around and sank his teeth in the life-giving food. "Ummmm," he grunted, as he tore chunks away from the bone. Then he moved to another leg.

There was a flurry of sand, a sharp "clash." The strong jaws of a trap clamped together on the toes of his hind foot. After one convulsive start, he stood still. Although the pain shot up his leg he remained motionless. "If I jump, I may step into another trap. Man has set these traps for me," he thought.

The Coyote remembered other animals who had been caught. He didn't go crazy. "Can I shake it off?" he wondered desperately. He pulled and tugged. "I'm caught," he thought, but kept pulling.

Weakened by lack of food, he was soon worn out. "There is only one thing to do," he knew. He turned and grimly chewed at the captured foot. In a moment the trap fell away. "I'm free," he thought, "and a few toes less are nothing."

Then the Coyote showed what a clever animal he is. "There is food here which I need," he thought. "If I'm careful I won't be caught again." So without moving, he ate as much of the sheep as he could reach. When he could hold no more, he considered the way to leave this dangerous place.

"If I crawl back over the same patch which I followed when I came, I shall be safe," he reasoned. Carefully, oh, so carefully, he backed away. Finally, when he had gone several yards, he decided, "It's safe." He turned and limped down a side arroyo toward his den.

The next day Mr. Brown rode by to see if he had caught anything. "Well, well," he observed to himself, "that Coyote has escaped again." The marks on the sand, the sprung trap, the three toes, and the track of the limping Coyote told the story.

Mr. Brown was disappointed, but at the same time said, "That Coyote is a sly pest but he is clever and he is stout-hearted. I guess he earned his freedom this time. But we'll see what he does the next time!"

And that is the way that Three-Toes received his nickname.

Keeping Alive

The long winter months dragged along. Though there was little snow, the cold air was keen and biting. All the little animals remained in their dens or shivered in the thorny mesquite thickets. Day after day Three-Toes grew hungrier and hungrier. Sometimes he was almost sure he would starve. Once he ate some old dry juniper berries which he found near the foothills.

For several days the Coyote had found nothing he could eat. He was hungrier than he had ever been before. "I'll go to the Brown Ranch," he

decided. "I know it's dangerous. But I must find something to eat or starve."

As Three-Toes approached the Brown Ranch he heard the dogs barking. "I must wait until the dogs have gone to sleep for the night," he thought. So he waited impatiently by the edge of the fence.

Finally everything was quiet. Three-Toes crept into the barn yard. He was noiseless as he slunk from one darkness into another. But the Coyote was disappointed. There seemed to be nothing he could eat.

He was slinking past a log cabin when he smelled it. "It smells like meat," he thought excitedly. "I'll follow the scent." Three-Toes crept around the building slowly and quietly. When he reached the other side the smell was much stronger. Going up close, he discovered that the door was ajar. The Coyote peered through the crack. Then he knew what the delicious smell was, for hanging from the rafter

was a half a beef. It was the cooking meat that was used for the Brown family.

"This looks dangerous," thought Three-Toes, "but I must eat." He decided to take a chance. So he went inside. "Um, um," the Coyote drooled, "what a feast!" The meat was just above his head. But by standing on his hind legs he could reach it. He began to tear at it ravenously. That set the beef swinging to and fro. He danced crazily about, stretched up tall, snatching a bite whenever he could.

The Coyote was so occupied with his good fortune that he forgot all about the fierce dogs. Suddenly he was startled by a noise in one of the corners. He gathered himself to run. "It's only mice," he decided and returned to his eating. Then the shed door creaked on its hinges. Instantly Three-Toes was at the doorway in one bound, all tensed to run. But it was only the wind moving the door.

"I really should leave," the Coyote told himself, feeling more uneasy. "I've been lucky to eat this much. But I'm still not full. Besides, the meat is so good." He began tearing at it again. Finally Three-Toes was really satisfied for the first time in many days. In fact, he was so full he could hardly move. Slowly he walked to the door. "I'll have to be very quiet and careful when I leave. I don't want the dogs to hear me," he thought. "I'm too full to run or fight!"

The Coyote listened intently before he ventured out of the cabin. He could hear the dogs growling. "Good," he thought, "the dogs are on the other side of the house." Quietly Three-Toes slipped out the door and slunk around the corner of the building. Creeping from shadow to shadow he was soon out on the mesa, AND SAFE.

Before long, he heard the dogs commence to bark furiously. "The dogs have scented my trail," he chuckled to himself. Three-Toes didn't mind now. He was happy. Once again he was full of good meat and too far away to be caught. He sat back on his haunches listening to the angry dogs and thought, "I fooled the dogs that time, and I'll fool them again and again."

Catching Rabbits

Even though the winter is long, there are always a few jack rabbits which manage to survive. The Coyote remembered them, for he was hungry again. He recalled their habits.

"I've noticed," he thought, "that when the Jack Rabbits leave their thicket, some Rabbits go down to the arroyo. Some have a favorite resting place under bushes where they stop. Some nibble bark on certain trees." Three-Toes, being crippled, couldn't run as fast as the Jack Rabbits, so he had to catch them by cunning.

That afternoon, Three-Toes decided to catch his supper by a trick. He ran along the top of a hill in plain sight of all the Rabbits. Then he hid. The Coyote knew the Rabbits would become uneasy when they saw him. He also knew that when he was out of sight they would worry all the more. They would wonder where he had gone, and where he was hiding. And, since they did not know, Three-Toes felt sure that the Rabbits would leave their mesquite thicket. He was certain that at least one Jack Rabbit would go down into the arroyo. That arroyo was well known to the Coyote. He remembered that there was a little side arroyo joining the main arroyo which the Rabbits used. That side arroyo was just the right place for him to hide. From there he could pounce upon an unsuspecting Rabbit.

So he concealed himself there and waited.

The longer Three-Toes remained out of sight the more uneasy the Rabbits became. They knew the Coyote would be where they least expected him. One by one they left the protection of the

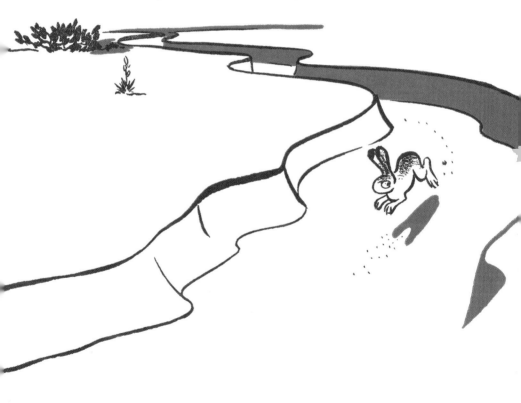

thorny thicket. Every Rabbit left, looking for a safer place to hide; a place away from the sharp eyes of the Coyote.

One old grey Jack Rabbit did just what Three-Toes had expected him to do. He hopped nervously right down into the arroyo. The Jack kept his eyes open, for he knew danger was near. He stayed away from every bush that might hide the Coyote. But the Jack Rabbit had forgotten about the side arroyo. The Coyote had sharp ears. He could hear the Rabbit coming. He was all ready to spring!

A little jay bird flew by overhead. She saw the Coyote. She realized that he was planning to pounce upon the Rabbit. Thinking she could warn the Jack Rabbit of his terrible danger, she began to shriek.

"Run! Run! Jack Rabbit!"

The old Jack Rabbit heard her. He knew then that the Coyote was nearby. But the poor frightened Jack Rabbit didn't know which way to run.

So he hesitated for a second trying to decide which way to go. That was a mistake. Three-Toes gave one big jump and had the Rabbit in his claws.

The little jay bird was horrified.

"ROBBER!

THIEF!!

COWARD!!!"

she screamed.

"Thank you, little bird," sneered the Coyote. "It was so nice of you to help me catch the Jack Rabbit."

The little bird had only meant to help the Rabbit. She was shocked at the result of her warning, but there was nothing she could do now. She fluffed up her feathers and flew away.

Three-Toes felt much better after he had finished his supper. He felt like singing. So he went to the top of the hill and, as the full moon came up, he began to bark and yip. He sounded like several animals as he howled.

"Yip, Yippy Yip, Yippy Yay
I'm a clever fellow, they say
Yip, Yippy Yip, Yippy Yay
Yip, Yippy Yip, Yippy Yay."

Then Three-Toes happened to think of the rabbit and sang:

"Yip, Yippy Yip, Yippy Yay
I caught a fine rabbit today
Yip, Yippy Yip, Yippy Yay
Yip, Yippy Yip, Yippy Yay."

A cowboy at the Brown Ranch heard the racket and remarked, "That old Coyote sounds mighty happy tonight. Guess I'll take a gun tomorrow and see if I can get a shot at him."

Three-Toes was happy. Tomorrow was another day and he didn't worry about it. For the moment his hunger was eased. The long cruel winter was nearly over. Soon spring would arrive and food would once more be plentiful. So he sang to the moon.

"Yip, Yippy Yip, Yippy Yay
Spring time is coming, hurray
Yip, Yippy Yip, Yippy Yay
Yip, Yippy Yip, Yippy Yay."